KEITH
THE CAT WITH THE MAGIC HAT

For Billy

SIMON AND SCHUSTER
First published in Great Britain in 2012
by Simon and Schuster UK Ltd
1st Floor, 222 Gray's Inn Road, London, WC1X 8HB
A CBS Company

A CIP catalogue record for this book is available
from the British Library upon request

978 0 85707 924 4 (HB)
978 1 47114 510 0 (PB)
978 0 85707 702 8 (eBook)

Printed in China
5 7 9 10 8 6

KEITH
THE CAT WITH THE MAGIC HAT

by Sue Hendra

SIMON AND SCHUSTER
London New York Sydney Toronto New Delhi

Keith the cat was merrily minding his own business when . . .

"Ha-ha-ha, Keith's got an ice cream stuck on his head!" chuckled the other cats.

Suddenly, Keith felt a little bit shy and a little bit silly.

"It's not an ice cream," he squeaked. "It's a . . .

It's a . . .

It's a . . .

It's a . . .

MAGIC HAT!
Yes, that's it!
A MAGIC HAT!"

This made the cats laugh even louder.
"Go on then, show us some magic!" they chortled.

Poor Keith! What was he going to do?
"W-w-well, first," stammered Keith,
 "I need my magic wand."

He reached for the chocolatey magic
wand on the ground but . . . .

It started to run away – ALL by itself!

The cats were amazed. "Wow, Keith! You made it move," they gasped.

Keith was amazed too . . . but he didn't say anything.
"More!" the cats cried, excitedly.
"More magic. More! More!"

Keith took a deep breath.
Then he waved his wand around . . .

"Abracadabra!"

But nothing happened.

Keith tried again.

"Alacazoo!"

Still nothing happened.

The cats were getting impatient.
They chanted and stamped their feet.
"MORE! MORE! MORE!"
"Whizzy-whoo-do-da!"
cried Keith AND . . .

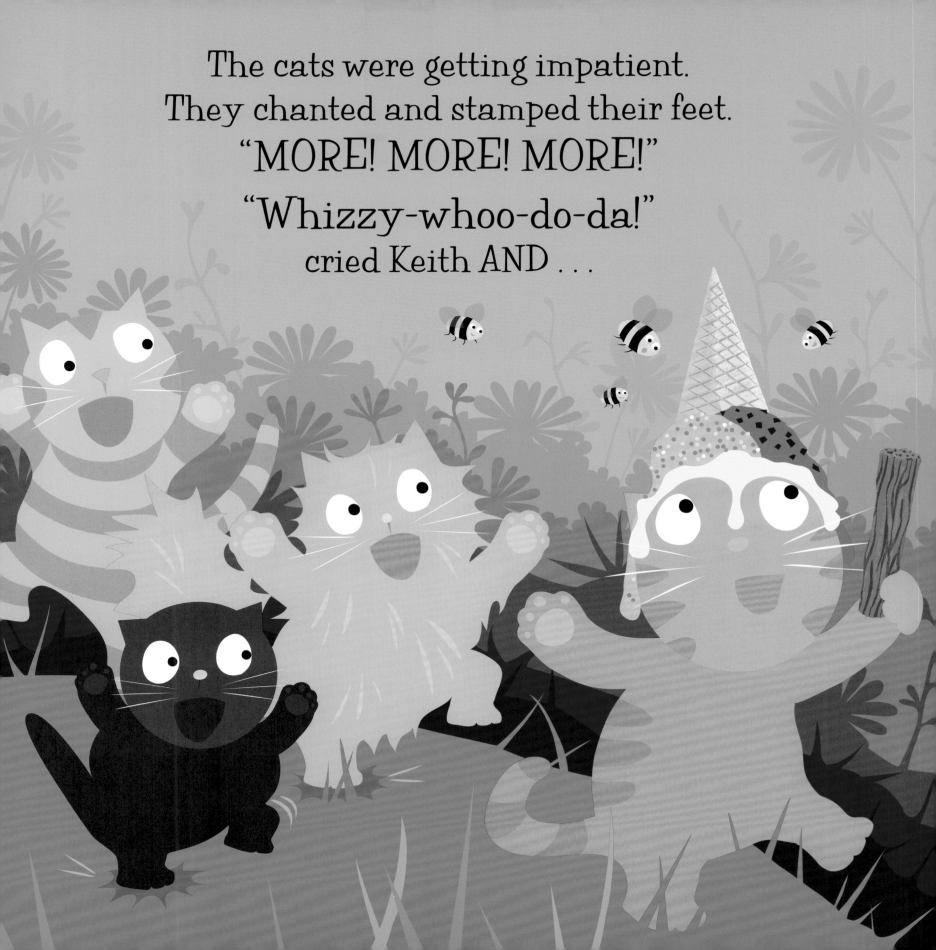

. . . just then, a whole family of rabbits popped out of the ground. They'd never heard such a noise!

"Keith – you did it!" the other cats cheered.
"You magicked up some rabbits. Hooray!"

They were all having such a fun time
that they didn't hear a distant WOOF!

WOOF! WOOF! WOOF!

But, of course, Keith couldn't REALLY do magic.
What was he going to do?

The cats ran up the tree.

They looked down at the barking dog. "Quick, Keith, do something!" they cried.

Then . . .

Whoops!

Keith's magic hat slipped off his head.
It was falling quickly through the air . . .

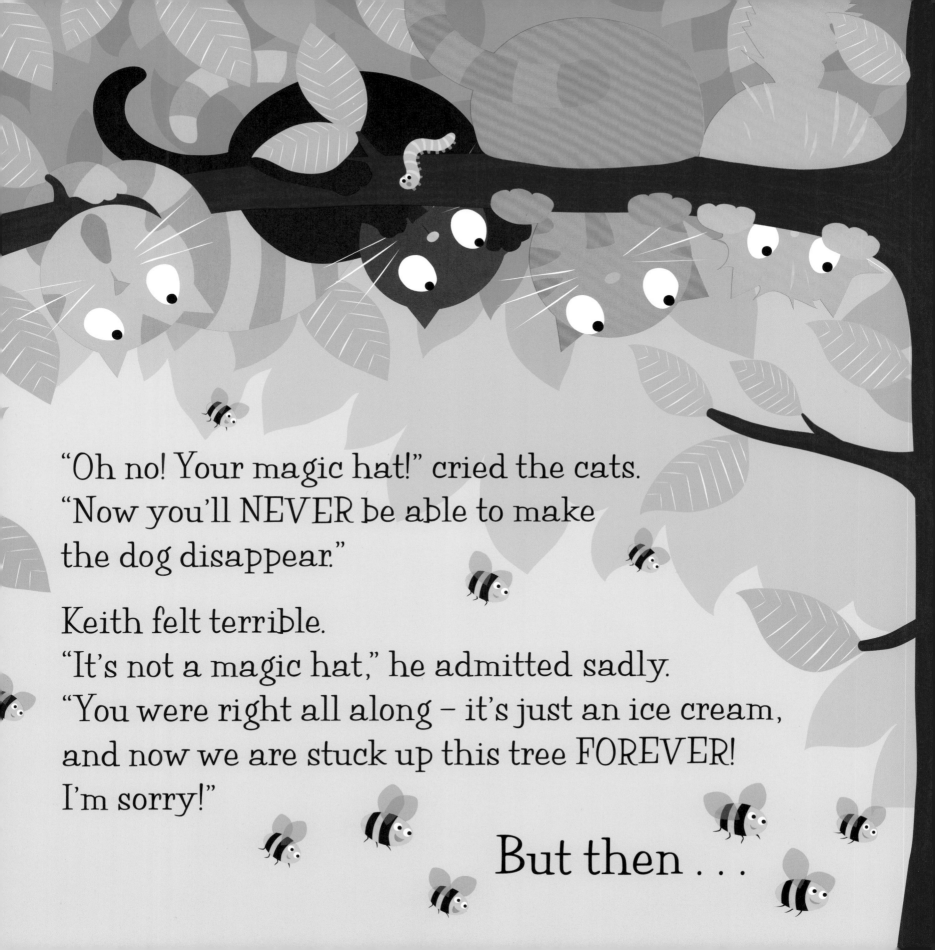

"Oh no! Your magic hat!" cried the cats.
"Now you'll NEVER be able to make
the dog disappear."

Keith felt terrible.
"It's not a magic hat," he admitted sadly.
"You were right all along – it's just an ice cream,
and now we are stuck up this tree FOREVER!
I'm sorry!"

But then . . .

"Hooray for Keith!" cried the cats.
"You're magic even without your hat!"
"Thank you," said Keith shyly. "And, for my
next trick, I will make this blob of ice cream
on the end of my nose disappear."

The cats waited patiently.

Then . . .

Keith stuck out his tongue and licked it off!

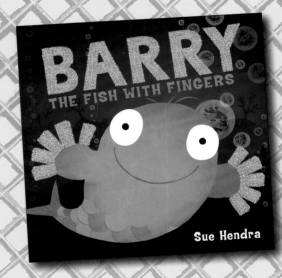

BARRY
THE FISH WITH FINGERS
Sue Hendra

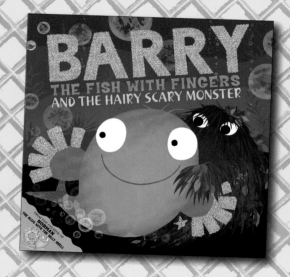

BARRY
THE FISH WITH FINGERS
AND THE HAIRY SCARY MONSTER

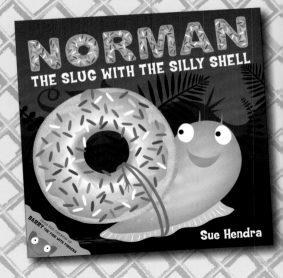

NORMAN
THE SLUG WITH THE SILLY SHELL
Sue Hendra

IF YOU LIKED THIS BOOK THERE ARE LOTS MORE BRILLIANT BOOKS BY SUE HENDRA FOR YOU TO ENJOY.

COME AND MAKE FRIENDS WITH ALL THE FANTASTIC CHARACTERS IN THE WONDERFUL WORLD OF SUE HENDRA!

www.worldofsuehendra.com

DOUG
THE BUG THAT WENT BOING!
Sue Hendra

NO-BOT
THE ROBOT WITH NO BOTTOM!
SUE HENDRA

SUPERTATO
Sue Hendra

Sue Hendra & Paul Linnet
I NEED A WEE!

NORMAN
THE SLUG WHO SAVED CHRISTMAS
Sue Hendra & Paul Linnet